Jamie Lee Curtis
&
Laura Cornell

JOANNA COTLER BOOKS

An Imprint of HarperCollins Publishers

Big Words
for Little People

Our BIG WORD is GRATITUDE to the TALENTED and SUPPORTIVE
Heidi Schaeffer, Phyllis Wender and Kelly Curtis, and the
INCOMPARABLE HarperCollins team: Karen Nagel, Alyson Day,
Carla Weise, Kathryn Silsand, Lucille Schneider and Dorothy Pietrewicz.

—J.L.C. & L.C.

Big Words for Little People
Text copyright © 2008 by Jamie Lee Curtis
Illustrations copyright © 2008 by Laura Cornell
Printed in the U.S.A.
For information address HarperCollins Children's Books,
a division of HarperCollins Publishers,
1350 Avenue of the Americas, New York, NY 10019.
www.harpercollinschildrens.com

Library of Congress Cataloging-in-Publication Data is available.
ISBN 978-0-06-112759-5 (trade bdg.) — ISBN 978-0-06-112760-1 (lib. bdg.)

Designed by Carla Weise
1 2 3 4 5 6 7 8 9 10
❖
First Edition

Little Words
for
Big People

For Joanna
—J.L.C. & L.C

I know some Big Words.
I'll teach them to you.
Although you are small,
you can use Big Words too.

aren't scary.
They're big fun to learn.
I was taught once
and now it's your turn.

If you need some time
to just be alone,
for doing weird dancing,
to sit still as a stone,
if someone is there
and you need to pee,
then say loud
and clear,

When Mommy can't fasten the brand-new car seat,
and the twins don't like what they got to eat—
"This is

impossible

Mom says to us. "Please!
We can't leave for school
till you help find the keys."

If you answer right when you spell a Big Word,
your teacher might shout,

"STUPENDOUS!
SUPERB!"

kingly

royal

gracefully

disappear

yodel

And then you can **CELEBRATE**—laugh and have fun—
'cause you've worked really hard to get the job done.

When you are at school
and you get into trouble
for chewing your gum,
then exploding a bubble,
and you stay inside
when your friends get to play,
your
CONSEQUENCE is
no recess that day.

When Dad takes us shopping
to buy new shoes,
and all of us shout,
"This one I choose!"

and the salesman looks angry—
he's pretty

IRATE—

When something is perfectly right for your age,
like TV and music, toys all the rage,
when a G-rated movie's the one that you seek,
APPROPRIATE is the word Mom will speak.

But many things are too old for you that lots of your friends may still get to do. **INAPPROPRIATE** is the word our mom picks if you want to watch PG-13 when you're six.

When you wait and you wait for your chance at a turn
and your feet are both hot and are starting to burn
and there's still
a long way to the
front of the line,

WORLD'S BIG WATER SLIDE

CHECK-IN

PATIENCE is the word you must try to find.

Mixing stuff up from the kitchen to drink
that looks really gross and has a big stink,
as our green-snotted brother's nose starts to get picked—

"DISGUSTING!"

you'd cry.
(It means yucky
and ick!)

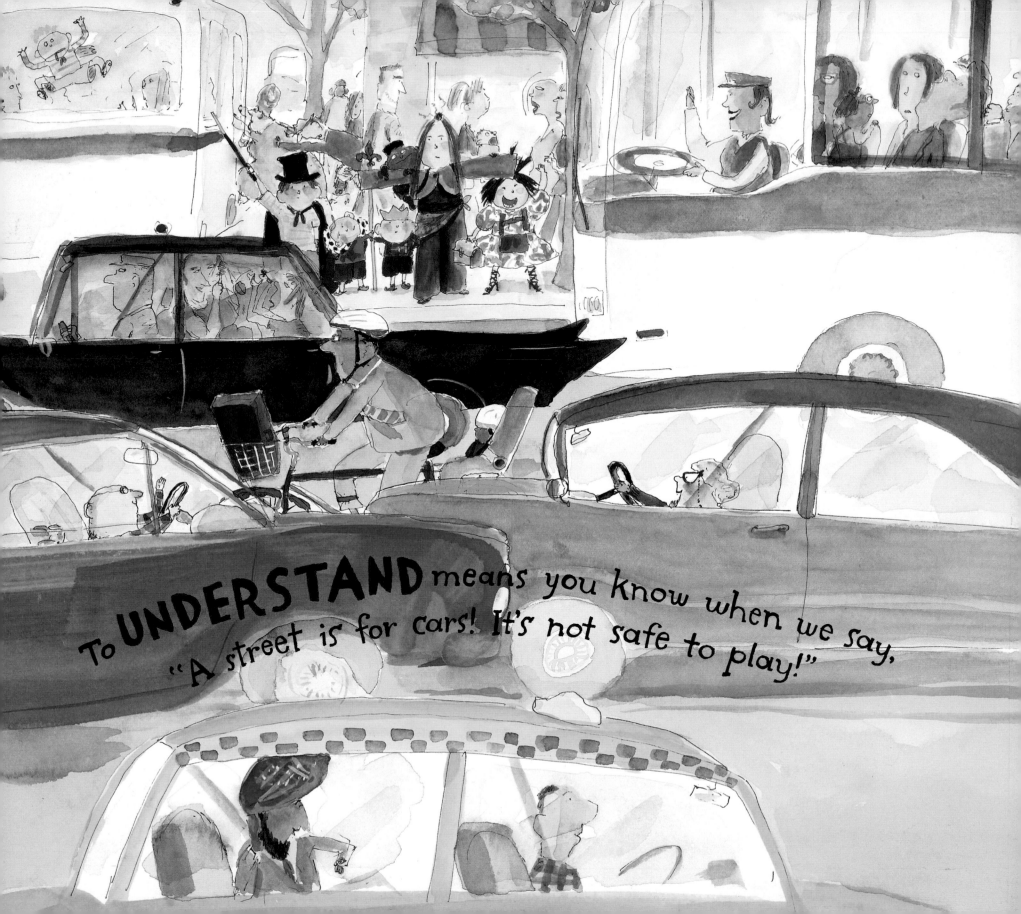

To **UNDERSTAND** means you know when we say, "A street is for cars! It's not safe to play!"

You understand
cows make milk and not juice,
that you don't run on "Duck"
but you do run on "Goose."

INCONSIDERATE
is the word Dad would pick
if you woke up Mom
when she's feeling sick.

But if you brought her
a flower and tea,
a **CONSIDERATE** person
is what he would see.

"I'm **RESPONSIBLE**," you say
when you pick up your toys

and walk our dog, Leo,
and try not to make noise.

Responsible people try not to forget
to water mom's bonsai or the table to set.

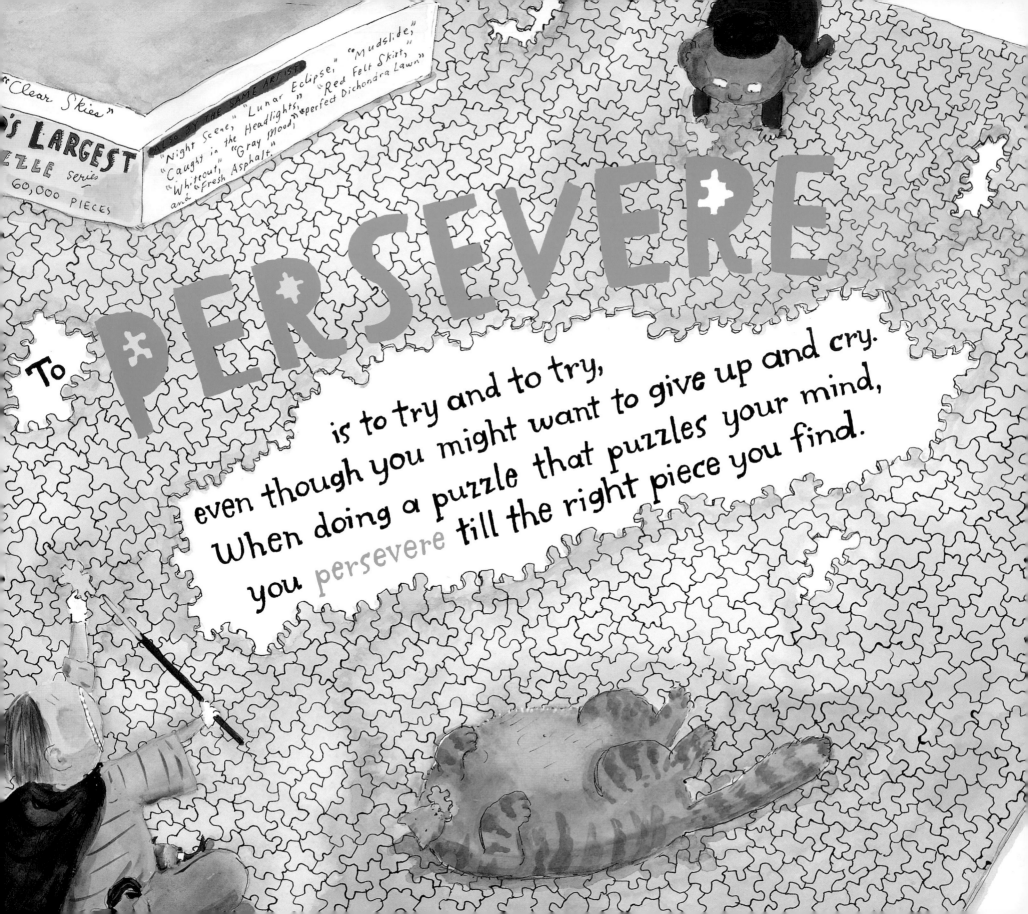

"Clear Skies"

'S LARGEST
EZZE series
60,000 PIECES

ALSO BY THE SAME ARTIST
"Night Scene," "Lunar Eclipse," "Mudslide,"
"Caught in the Headlights," "Red Felt Skirt,"
"Whiteout," "Gray Mood," "perfect Dichondra Lawn"
and "Fresh Asphalt."

To PERSEVERE

is to try and to try,
even though you might want to give up and cry.
When doing a puzzle that puzzles your mind,
you persevere till the right piece you find.

DIFFERENT means nobody's ever the same.

All bodies are **different** and so are all brains.

Different is what makes this world so great.

Different is never something to hate.

But not all **Big Words**
are as **long** as the rest.
There are three—
though short—
that I love the best.

FAMILY is where we all belong,
keeping us safe, making us strong.
Family is yours, no matter—whatever!—
we care about you forever and ever.

RESPECT is the way we all treat each other—
mother to father, father to mother,

brother to sister,

sister to brother,

and brother

and sister

and sister

and brother...

Love

is the biggest **BIG** word of all.
Four little letters that help you walk tall.
Love is your family, your siblings, your friends.
Love is your ocean without any end.

See, Big Words are easy. How well you've done!
Now go off and have some really great fun.
And next time a grown-up thinks you don't have sense,
show them with Big Words your

INTELL

IGENCE!